King of Prussia Frederick II

Origin of the Bismarck Policy

The Hohenzollern doctrine and maxims described

King of Prussia Frederick II

Origin of the Bismarck Policy
The Hohenzollern doctrine and maxims described

ISBN/EAN: 9783337382643

Printed in Europe, USA, Canada, Australia, Japan

Cover: Foto ©Andreas Hilbeck / pixelio.de

More available books at **www.hansebooks.com**

ORIGIN

OF THE

BISMARCK POLICY:

OR,

THE HOHENZOLLERN DOCTRINE AND MAXIMS

DESCRIBED AND DEFINED

BY THE MOST EMINENT MONARCH OF THE PRUSSIAN DYNASTY,

FREDERIC THE GREAT:

HIS OPINIONS ON RELIGION, JUSTICE, MORALS, POLITICS,
DIPLOMACY, STATESMANSHIP, THE GERMAN
PEOPLE, &c., &c.

WRITTEN BY HIMSELF EXPRESSLY FOR THE USE OF
HIS SUCCESSOR TO THE THRONE.

Carefully Translated from an Authentic Copy of the Original MS.
By M. C. L.

BOSTON:
CROSBY & DAMRELL, 100 WASHINGTON STREET.
1870.

REMARKS.

1. At this time, when Prussia attracts the attention of the whole world, this publication of a very curious work of Frederic II.* can hardly fail to interest the public.

2. These pages were written by that king for the instruction and guidance of his nephew and successor to the throne, and are the opinions which the greatest and most celebrated sovereign of the Hohenzollern dynasty entertained on Religion, Justice, Morals, Politics, Statesmanship, the German People, etc., etc.

3. The Translator and Editor, and the Publishers, wish it to be well understood that they do not, of course, hold themselves in the least responsible for the sentiments, doc-

---

* Frederic II., third king of Prussia, generally called Frederic the Great, was born in Berlin, Jan. 24, 1712, and died at the château of Sans-Souci, Aug. 17, 1786.

His biographers say that he was very careless about his dress and personal appearance; and that, when he died, he had not a single decent shirt, and his valet had to lend him one to be buried in ! — TRANSLATOR'S NOTE.

trines, and principles set forth or professed by the AUTHOR of this work, but leave all the responsibility to whom it belongs.

4. The translation has been made as literal as possible. Therefore, as the style and language used by King Frederic in his writings are often inelegant, and sometimes rather ambiguous and obscure, the English will likewise be occasionally found somewhat inelegant, because the translator, unwilling to alter the sense of the original, has faithfully adhered to the very ideas and phraseology of the author.

5. A few explanatory, historical, and biographical notes have been added by the TRANSLATOR.

INSTRUCTIONS

OF

FREDERIC II. OF PRUSSIA

TO

HIS SUCCESSOR TO THE CROWN.

I.

The Origin of our House.

In the times of disorder and confusion, a new form of sovereignty sprang from the midst of the barbaric nations. The governors of the different provinces shook off the yoke; and, having soon become sufficiently powerful to intimidate their masters, they obtained privileges, or rather, by apparent submissiveness and allegiance, they attained their desired ends.

Several of these bold reformers laid the foundations of the strongest and greatest monarchies; and perhaps, even, /if we take every thing into consideration. all the reigning emperors, kings, and princes owe their thrones and dominions to them.

In fact, that has surely been the case with us. You blush at that, my dear nephew! Well, you are excusable; but take care not to be so childish henceforth, and always bear in mind, that, with regard to kingdoms, we monarchs take what we can, when we can; and we are never in the wrong, except when compelled to give up what we. had taken.

Tavillon,* Count of Hohenzollern, was the first among our own ancestors who acquired any right of sovereignty in the countries which he governed; the thirteenth of his descendants had the title of Burgrave of Nuremberg; the twenty-fifth was the Elector of Brandenburg; and the thirty-seventh, king of Prussia.

Like all the others, our dynasty has had its

---

* Frederic uses the name *Tavillon,* yet many biographies have *Thassilo.* — *Note of the Translator.*

architects, Ciceros, Nestors, and Neros; its fools
and idlers; its learned women, its cruel moth-
ers, and, very surely, its coquettes and licentious
women.

Our house has also often been enlarged by
those rights which belong only to fortunate or
all-powerful monarchs; for there are to be seen
only those of conveniency, abeyance, and pro-
tection, in the order of our successions to the
throne.

From the time of Tavillon to that of the
great Elector, our house was hardly able to sup-
port itself.

There were fifty princes in the Empire who
were our equals in every respect; and, properly
speaking, we were ourselves only a branch of
the great empire of Germany.

William the Great, by his bold and dashing
exploits, raised us from our obscure condition;
and finally, in 1701, — not very long ago, as you
see, — vanity placed a regal crown on my grandfather's head. We can trace the beginning of
our true grandeur to that very time, since it
gives me the privilege to argue as a king, and

to negotiate on an equal footing with all the powers and governments in the world.

If we should sum up the virtues of our ancestors, we would easily discover that the aggrandizement of our house is not due to such advantages. Most of our royal ancestors proved to be very bad characters.

But chance and circumstances have greatly favored us. I especially wish you to observe that our first diadem was placed on a vain and frivolous head, belonging to a crooked and distorted body. I know very well, my dear nephew, that I leave you in perfect uncertainty and doubt concerning our true origin. They pretend that the Count of Hohenzollern belonged to a great and illustrious family; but, in reality, no one assumed fewer titles than he did.

On the Geographical Situation of my Kingdom.

I am not very well favored in that respect; and, to convince yourself of the fact, cast your eyes on a map, and you will see that the various parts of my kingdom are divided in such a manner as not to be able to afford mutual assistance to each other.

No large rivers flow through my provinces: a few border them, but hardly any transect them.

On the Nature of the Soil of my Provinces.

Fully one-third of my kingdom lies fallow; and another third is composed of forests, rivers, and marshes. The part which is cultivated produces neither wine, nor olive-trees, nor mulberry-trees: fruits and vegetables are raised only by dint of care and great labor, and very few of them are perfectly good.

I have only a few counties where rye and wheat of some reputation are raised.

Concerning the Customs and Habits of the Inhabitants.

I cannot express any decided opinion on that subject, as my kingdom is composed of different provinces, — pieced together, so to say. All I can affirm as certain is, that, in general, all my subjects are brave and sturdy; not very epicurean, but great drunkards; tyrants in their own lands and homes, and slaves in my army; dull and insipid lovers, and brutal husbands; endowed with a *sang froid* which, after all, I think, is nothing but stupidity.   They are well versed in jurisprudence, very poor philosophers, miserable orators, and still worse poets.   They affect a great simplicity in their attire, but think they are quite well dressed when they have a small purse, a large hat, cuffs a yard long, boots reaching to their waist, a small cane, a very short coat, and a very long waistcoat.

.   .   .   .

NOTE. — A short paragraph on the women is here omitted by the translator on account of the impropriety of the language used in it. — *Translator's note.*

II.

On Religion.

RELIGION is absolutely necessary in a State government. The discussion of that maxim would be very impolitic, and a king is wrong when he allows his subjects to carry such discussions to excess. But, on the other hand, it is unwise for a king to have a religion.

Mark this well, my dear nephew: there is nothing which tyrannizes over the mind and heart so much as religion, because it agrees neither with our passions, nor with the high political views which a monarch should entertain.

If a king fears God, or, in better words, *future punishment*, he becomes bigoted like a monk. If a favorable opportunity of taking forcible possession of a neighboring province is offered, immediately an army of demons seems to him ready to defend it: he is weak-minded enough to think he is going to commit an injustice, and he proportions the punishment of his crime to the extent of his evil designs.

When he is about to conclude a treaty with some foreign power, if he only remembers that he is a Christian, all is lost: he will always suffer himself to be duped or imposed upon.

With regard to war, it is a business in which the slightest scruple spoils the whole matter. In fact, where can an honest man be found willing to carry on a war, if he had not the right to make regulations justifying pillage, incendiarism, and carnage?

However, I do not mean to say that impiety is to be openly displayed; but we must adapt our thoughts to our rank and standing in the world.

All the popes who have had common sense enough adopted systems of religion consistent with their ambitious designs, and it would be the height of folly, if a monarch's attention was diverted by trifles which are fit only for the common people.

Besides, the most complete indifference for religious matters is the best means which a king can have to prevent his subjects from becoming fanatics.

Believe me, my dear nephew, the Church has her little whims and fancies like any one else. Strive, therefore, to regard the matter as a true philosopher, and you will see that no disputes of importance on religion will take place in your kingdom ; for factions are formed only because of the want of firmness and decision on the part of monarchs and their ministers.

An important remark, worthy of your consideration, is that your ancestors acted in a most sensible manner on this subject: they undertook a reform which gave them an air of apostles, while at the same time they filled their treasury. It is undoubtedly the most rational change which ever occurred in this kind of matter. But since there is almost nothing left to be gained now, and as it would, moreover, be dangerous to follow in their footsteps, we must keep within the bounds of tolerance.

Remember the following precept well, my dear nephew, and always say, as I do, " *In my kingdom, people pray as they wish, and find their salvation as they can;"* for, if you seem to neglect that maxim ever so little, every thing will be lost for you in your kingdom.

Here is the reason why my kingdom is composed of different religious sects. The Reformed hold almost all the offices in certain provinces, whilst, in others, the Lutherans enjoy the same privileges. There are some provinces in which the Catholics predominate to such an extent that the king can send but one or two Protestant commissioners there. As for the Jews, they are poor creatures, who generally are not so much in the wrong as they are said to be. They pay their taxes promptly, and, after all, cheat none but foolish people.

Since our ancestors became Christians in the new century to please the emperors, Lutherans in the fifteenth to possess themselves of the property of the Church, and Reformers in the sixteenth to be agreeable to the Dutch, we can certainly act differently in order to maintain tranquillity and peace in our States.

My father had an excellent project in view, but it proved a failure. He had induced President Laon to write for him a little treatise on religion to try to unite the three sects together.

The president spoke against the pope, called St. Joseph an old fool, pulled St. Roch's dog by the ears, and St. Anthony's pig by the tail [i.e. spoke irreverently of them. — *Translator's note*].

He did not believe in St. Susan's chastity, and regarded St. Bernard and St. Dominick as courtiers. He disowned St. Francis de Sales. He had no more respect for the eleven thousand virgins than for the saints and martyrs of the Loyola family. As for the holy mysteries, he agreed that no attempts should be made to explain them, but that common sense should prevail in every particular, and that the literal meaning of words should not too strictly be adhered to.

With regard to the Lutherans, he used them as his *fulcrum :* he wanted the Catholics to become somewhat unfaithful to the court of Rome; but he also demanded of the Lutherans that they should be less subtile in disputes; and he maintained, that, provided some distinctions were removed, he was certain all the creeds would very nearly come to the same.

It was thought President Laon would have more trouble in reconciling the Calvinists, because they had greater claims than the Lutherans. However, he proposed a good expedient in the matter of the great difficulty of having no one but God for a confidant when preparing for communion.

He regarded the worship of images as an al lurement for the common people, and he thought a peasant should have some kind of saint.

As for the monks, he expelled them as enemies who require great contributions.

Regarding the priests, he wanted them to marry housekeepers. This created a great sensation; for the good ladies pretended they were injured, and that it would be a sacrilege to interfere with the holy mysteries.

Had this pamphlet been well received, every effort would have been made to carry out the plan which had been formed. For my part, I have not quite given it up. I even hope to afford you facility enough to put it through.

Here is what I am doing for that. I am trying to induce all writers in my kingdom to spread through their writings a contempt for all those who have been reformers; and I never miss the slightest opportunity of developing the ambitious views of the court of Rome, and of the priests and ministers. I will gradually accustom my subjects to think as I do, and I will make them give up all prejudices; but, as they must have some form of worship, I will find out, if I live long enough, some eloquent man who will preach a new creed.

At first, I will feign to be willing to persecute him, but I will gradually declare in his favor, and will heartily embrace his system.

This system, if you want me to tell you, is already prepared. Voltaire * has composed the preamble of it. He proves the necessity of giving up all that has hitherto been said about religion, because people do not agree on any point.

_____

* VOLTAIRE (*François M. Arouet de*) was born at Châtenay, near Paris, Feb. 20, 1694; died in Paris, May 30, 1778. Frederic II. opened a correspondence with him, Aug. 8, 1736; and in July, 1750, Voltaire, at the invitation of Frederic, went to Prussia, where he was on the most intimate terms with that king, who conferred the highest honors upon him. But, having had quarrels, Voltaire left the court of Berlin forever, on the 26th of March, 1753. — *Translator's note.*

Voltaire describes each sectarian leader with a freedom which resembles plain truth. He has hunted up devout men, popes, bishops, priests, and ministers, by which a queer gayety is spread all over his work, which is written in such a concise and flowing style, that it leaves no time for reflection ; and, like an orator skilled in the most subtle art, he seems in very good earnest while proclaiming the most doubtful principles.

D'Alembert* and Maupertuis † have traced the outline of this new religion : they have ar-

---

* D'ALEMBERT *(Jean Le Rond)* was born in Paris, Nov. 16, 1717; died 1783.   Versed in mathematics and literature, he was one of the most celebrated philosophers of his times.   He was unanimously received as a member of the Berlin Academy in 1746; and Frederic II. offered him the presidency of that institution, but D'Alembert declined the honor.

† MAUPERTUIS *(Pierre L. Moreau de)*, a French philosopher and geometer, and author of several esteemed works, was born at St. Malo, July 17, 1698, died at Basle, July 27, 1759.   He went to Prussia in May, 1740, and was very warmly received by the king, whom he accompanied in the Silesian campaign.   Maupertuis was taken prisoner at the battle of Molwitz, but was soon set at liberty by the Austrians, who treated him with great respect.   In 1744, he returned to Berlin, when he married Mlle. de Borck, one of the ladies of that court.   Frederic appointed him to the presidency of the Berlin Academy, made him a knight of the Order of Merit, bestowed upon him an annual pension of 15,000 francs, and gave him all the rights of a native citizen of Prussia. — *Translator's notes.*

ranged it with so much care and precision that one might be tempted to believe that they have tried to demonstrate it to each other before attempting to demonstrate it to the public.

Rousseau * has been laboring, for the last four years, to anticipate every possible objection. I expect a great deal of pleasure in mortifying all those lordlings and stiff ministers who may dare to gainsay us.

There is already prepared a series of fifty consequences for each subject of controversy, and of at least thirty reflections upon each article of the Holy Scriptures. Rousseau is even presently engaged in proving that all what is written now-a-days is nothing but fables; that there never was a terrestrial Paradise, and that it is degrading God to believe that he has made his image a perfect dunce, and his most perfect creature a true libertine: for, after all, he adds, it is only the length of the serpent's tail which can have

---

* ROUSSEAU (Jean Jacques), an eloquent French writer and renowned philosopher, was born at Geneva, June 28, 1712; died at Ermenonville, near Paris, July 2, 1778. His literary career is one of the most brilliant and distinguished, and is too well known to need any further notice here. — Translator's note.

seduced Eve; and, if such be the case, it would prove a frightful disorder in the imagination.

The Marquis d' Argens * and Mesdames de Formey have prepared the organization of the Council. I am to preside over it, but without presuming that the Holy Spirit will give more wisdom to me than to the others.

There will be only one minister from each sect, and four deputies from each province, two of whom belonging to the nobility, and two to the *tiers-état*. All the rest of the priests, monks, and ministers shall be excluded from the Council, as interested parties in the case; and, that the Holy Ghost may better seem to preside over this assembly, we will agree to make decisions only according to common sense.

---

* *Marquis* D'ARGENS *(Jean B. Boyer)* was born at Aix, June 24, 1704, and died Jan. 11, 1771. He was the author of numerous philosophical and other works. He became acquainted with Frederic II. when the latter was only Prince Royal. After the death of Frederic I., D'Argens went to Potsdam, where he was heartily welcomed. The king gave him the title of Lord Chamberlain, and a pension of 6000 francs, and made him Director-General of the Department of *belles-lettres* in the Academy. — *Translator's note.*

III.

On Justice.

We owe justice to our subjects as they owe us respect, — that is granted ; but it is necessary to take care that we are not brought under subjection by justice itself.

Let us picture to ourselves, my dear nephew, the unfortunate Charles the First being led to the scaffold. I am by nature too ambitious to be willing that there should exist in my kingdom any instituted power which might restrain me. It was this very sentiment which solely induced me to make a new code of laws. I know very well that I banished the good goddess ; but I was rather afraid of her sharp eyes, because I know how much influence she has among the common people, and I also knew that skilful princes, while satisfying their ambition, can often make themselves adored.

The majority of my subjects believed I had

been moved with compassion on beholding the
misfortunes which are engendered by chicanery.
Alas! I confess it to you, and I almost blush at
it, far from having had that in view, I regret
the little advantages which it procured to me;
for the taxes established on legal proceedings
and stamped paper have diminished my income
by nearly *five hundred thousand florins.*

Do not allow yourself to be dazzled, my dear
nephew, by the word *justice :* it is a word which
has different relations, and which can be ex-
plained in different ways. Here is the meaning
which I attach to it : —

Justice is the image of God. Who can therefore attain to so high a perfection? Is not man
unreasonable when he undertakes the vain project of having full possession of it? Behold all
the countries in the world, and examine if justice
is administered exactly in the same manner in
two kingdoms. Consider, after that, the different principles which govern men, and see if they
agree.

Is it, therefore, surprising that every one
wishes to be just in his own way?

When I undertook to look into all the courts of justice in my kingdom, I found an immense army, legions of honest people, often too much suspected not to be such. Each court had another above itself: I myself had my own ; and I was not vexed by that, because it was a custom.

On examining the progress which justice was making in my dominions, I was frightened to see, that, one hundred years hence, one-tenth part of my subjects would be engaged in the administration of justice ; and, on calculating that those legions would have to be paid and provided for, I shuddered when I saw that the tenth part of my State revenues would pass into their hands.

But what gave me the most anxiety was that sure and steady way of proceeding which lawyers have, that sense of freedom which is inseparable from their principles, and that clever manner of preserving their advantages under the appearances of the strictest equity and justice.

I pondered over all the energetic, but often queer doings of the Parliaments of England and of Paris.

Although I admired them, I was sometimes ashamed for the dignity of the throne.

It was in the midst of these reflections that I decided to undermine the foundations of that great power, justice; and it has only been by simplifying it as much as I could, that I have brought it down to the point where I wanted it to be.

You may perhaps be surprised, my dear nephew, that unarmed people, who never talk but with respect of the king's sacred person, should be the only ones capable of dictating to him. It is precisely for those very reasons that it is not difficult for them to clog our power. They can never be suspected of using violent measures, because they are unarmed; neither could they be accused of being disrespectful towards us, since they always talk to us with the utmost deference and *decorum;* and our subjects are very soon persuaded by that powerful eloquence which seems to be produced only for their happiness and our glory.

I have reflected a great deal upon the advantages which a kingdom derives from a body which represents the whole nation, and is the guardian of its laws; I even think that a king is more sure of his crown when law gives it to him or keeps it for him; but a monarch must be a very worthy man, and well imbued with good principles, to allow his actions to be daily scrutinized.

When he is ambitious, he must not permit it. I could never have done any thing, had I been under restraint. I might have passed for a just monarch, but they would refuse me the title of a hero.

IV.

On Policy.

As it has been agreed among men that to cheat our fellow-creatures is a base and criminal act, it has been necessary to find a word which might modify the idea; and the word *policy* has been sanctioned to that end. In all probability, this word was selected only for sovereigns, because they cannot really be called rogues or rascals.

However that may be, here is what I think of policy. I mean, by the word *policy*, that we must always try to dupe other people: that is the means, not of getting the advantage, but of remaining on an equal footing; for be sure that all the governments in the world have the same end in view.

This principle being laid down, do not be ashamed of making interested alliances from which only you yourself can derive the whole advantage. Do not make the foolish mistake of not breaking them when you believe that your interests require it; and, above all, uphold the following maxim: "That to despoil your neighbors is to deprive them of the means of injuring you."

Policy, properly speaking, establishes and perpetuates kingdoms; and consequently, my dear nephew, policy should be well comprehended, conceived, and understood with regard to great interests. To this end, we are going to divide it into statesmanship and private policy.

The former concerns only the higher interests of the kingdom; the latter is for the use of the monarch.

V.

On Private Policy.

A prince must show only the better side of his character: that is to what you must apply yourself in good earnest, my dear nephew. When I was the Prince Royal, I was a very poor soldier: I liked my own comfort and convenience, good cheer, and good wine, and I was always headlong in love.

When I became a king, I appeared to be a soldier, a philosopher, and a poet. I ate coarse bread like my soldiers, drank very little wine in the presence of my subjects, and feigned to regard women with contempt.

The following is the course I have adopted in all my actions.

VI.

About my Travelling.

I always walk without any escort; and, day and night, I go on my way without any military display. My suite is not numerous, but very select; my carriage is quite plain in appearance, but it is perfectly easy and commodious, so that I sleep in it as comfortably as in my bed.

I appear to pay very little attention to my manner of living: a footman, a cook, and a pastry-cook are all the servants I require to wait upon me. I order my dinner myself: and that is not the worst thing I do, because I know all about the country where I am travelling; and I ask for the best game, fish, or meats which it affords.

When I arrive at a place, I appear tired, and I show myself to the crowd in a great-coat and an uncombed wig. These things are trifles which often produce strange impressions.

I give audience to everybody, excepting priests, monks, and ministers. As those gentlemen are used to speaking from a distance, I listen to their speeches from my window, and one of my footmen receives them at the door and presents my compliments to them.

In all that I say, I always appear to think of nothing but my subjects' happiness. I ask questions of noblemen, tradesmen, and workmen, and I converse with them on the least topics.

You must have heard as well as myself, my dear nephew, the flattering remarks of those good people: remember the man who said I must be very kind to give myself so much trouble after such a long and wearisome war. And remember, also, the one who pitied me from the bottom of his heart on seeing my threadbare overcoat, and the small dishes served up at my table. The poor man was not aware that I had a nice coat underneath; and he thought people could not live if they had not a whole ham or a quarter of veal for dinner.

VII.

The Reviewing of my Troops.

Before reviewing a regiment, I take care to read the names of all the officers and sergeants; and I commit to memory three or four of them, with the name of the company to which they belong.

I take care to be strictly informed of the little wrongs and abuses committed by the captains, and I allow the soldiers to complain to me personally.

The hour appointed for the review arrives. I start from my quarters: very soon a crowd surrounds me, and I do not allow any one to disperse it. I talk with the man who stands nearest to me, and who makes the best answers to my questions.

When I have reached the regiment, I make it manœuvre. I pass through the ranks slowly, and talk to every captain : when I am opposite those whose names I have remembered, I call them out, as well as their lieutenants and sergeants; and that gives me the appearance of having a good deal of memory and reflection.

You saw, my dear nephew, the manner in which I humbled that major who used to furnish the soldiers in his company with shirts much too short for them. I managed the affair so well that one of the soldiers had the boldness to pull his shirt out of his breeches to show everybody it was really too short.

When a regiment manœuvres badly, I have my own way of punishing it. I give orders for it to drill two weeks longer, and I do not invite any of the officers to dine with me.

If the regiment manœuvres very well, I allow all the captains, and even a few of the lieutenants, to eat with me.

By thus passing reviews, I become thoroughly acquainted with my troops; and, when I find an officer who answers all my questions clearly and straightforwardly, I put his name on my list, so that I may remember him when opportunity requires.

To this day, every one believes that the great love I have for my subjects induces me to visit the different parts of my kingdom as often as I can. I let every one remain under that impression, although this is not my real motive. The fact is, I am obliged to act thus; and here is the reason why.

My government is a despotic one; consequently, he who rules over the kingdom has the exclusive charge of it. If I did not travel over my States, my governors would take my place, and would gradually dispense with the principles of obedience, to adopt only those of independence. Besides, as my orders cannot be otherwise than imperious and peremptory, those who represent me would assume the same tyrannical tone; whilst, by occasionally travelling through my kingdom, I have the means of discovering the abuse which they make of the power that I have delegated to them, and of recalling to their duty and admonishing those who might be tempted to depart from it. Add to those reasons that of making my subjects believe that I come into their country to listen to their complaints, and to relieve them from their troubles.

8

VIII.

On Belles-Lettres.

I have made great exertions to acquire a literary reputation. I have been more fortunate than Cardinal Richelieu; for, thank God, I am regarded as an author. But, *entre-nous*, wits are a queer kind of people : they are insufferably vain. Many a poet would refuse my kingdom if he were obliged to give up to me two of his finest lines.

As it is a trade which is incompatible with regal occupations, I compose only when I have nothing more important to do ; and, that I may give myself a little more ease, I have at my court a few *literati* who are intrusted with the care of arranging and writing down my ideas.

You saw with how much distinction I treated D'Alembert when he came to Prussia. I always had him at table with me, and I did nothing but praise him constantly. You appeared surprised that I had so much regard for that author. Do you not know, then, that this philosopher is listened to as an oracle in Paris, and that he never speaks but of my talents and virtues, and that he maintains everywhere that I have the character and disposition of a hero and a great king ?

Moreover, it is very sweet for me to hear myself praised with judgment and distinction ; and, to tell you the truth, I am very far from being indifferent to praise.

I know very well that all my actions must not have reference to that ; but D'Alembert is so polite when he is with me, that he never speaks except to say the most agreeable and obliging things to me.

Voltaire had not the same disposition ; so I dismissed him. I boasted of it in the Academy, as a meritorious deed ; but, in reality, I feared Voltaire, because I was not sure of always being able to treat him as well, and I had an instinctive feeling that any retrenchment from my liberalities would bring upon me thousands of sarcasms.

Besides, after taking all things into consideration, and consulting with my Academy, it was decided that two distinguished wits can never live together harmoniously.

I forgot to tell you, that, in the midst of my greatest misfortunes, I always took care to pay my *literati* their pensions.

Philosophers consider war as a most abominable folly as soon as it interferes with their own interests.

IX.

Conduct in Minute Details.

Would you learn how to please everybody at little expense ? Here is the secret of that. Permit all your subjects to write to you directly and speak to you personally ; and when you answer them, verbally or otherwise, you must use this language : " If what you communicate to me is true, I will do you justice ; but rely also upon the zeal with which I have always punished calumny and falsehood. I am your king (signed), FREDERIC."

If any one should come to complain, listen attentively to him, or with an air which may induce him to think you do so. Especially, let your answer be firm and laconic. Two letters written in that style, and a couple of answers of that sort, will spare you the annoyance of complaints ; and in your States, and still more in foreign courts, will give you an air of simplicity and *minutiæ*, which is of the highest importance for monarchs. I know, my dear nephew, that to two such letters which the French took from me in 1757 I owe the reputation in which I have been held by that nation of being the most unaffected, most popular, and equitable of kings.

X.

On Dress.

Had my grandfather lived twenty years longer, we might have been ruined, because his birthdays would have exhausted the whole of our kingdom's revenues.

I never wear any thing else but my military uniform. The army believe that I do so on account of the great esteem I have for their profession, and I leave them under that impression ; but, in truth, it is to give them the example. My father was perfectly right in adopting blue coats for gala days. When men are not rich, and want to dress well, they must adopt a full military costume.

XI.

Of Pleasures.

Love is a god who spares no one: when we resist the darts which he shoots openly, he changes his tactics. Thus, take my word for it, do not be vain enough to try to resist him: he will always outwit you.

Although I have no reason to complain of the tricks he has played upon me, I advise you, however, not to follow my example. It might, in course of time, produce evil results: all your governors and officers would live rather for their pleasures than for your glory, and very soon your army would act as your uncle Henry's regiment.

I would have been fond of hunting, but the accounts of your grandfather's master of the hounds took that fancy from my head. My father told me many a time, that there were only two kings in Europe wealthy enough to hunt the stag, because it is unbecoming for a crowned head to go hunting like a mere nobleman.

Nature has endowed me with rather moderate tastes and inclinations. I am fond of good cheer, — wine, coffee, and liquors; and yet my subjects think I am the most temperate prince in the world. When I dine in public, my German cook caters for me. I drink beer, and two or three glasses of wine in the course of the meal. When I am in my private apartment, my French cook does all he can to satisfy me; and I confess I am rather hard to please. Here I am near my bed, so that I am not uneasy about what I drink.*

Notwithstanding what philosophers say, the senses deserve that we should devote two hours daily to their gratification; and, really, what would our life be without the senses? I enjoy pleasures, but I never could accustom myself to lose by them.

Gaming is the mirror of the soul; which is

---

* He means he does not care about the quality or quantity he drinks, because, if he takes too much, his bed is near by, and there he can sleep off the effects of his potations privately. — *Translator's note.*

not exactly what I want, because I am not at all anxious that everybody should see my secret thoughts and feelings.

Consequently, my dear nephew, examine yourself well; and, if you have no decided inclination for gambling, you can play.

I like theatrical performances very much, and music above all; but I think an opera troupe is very expensive, and the pleasure I derive from hearing a fine singer, or a talented violinist, would be far greater if it did not cost me quite so much money. As no one under-estimates that expense, I have done my best to prove that it is a necessary expenditure; but the old generals could never understand why a clown or a musician should receive the same pay as they have.

My dear nephew, I here make man known at my own expense; and I assure you that he is always given up to his passions, that he glories in self-conceit, and that all his virtues rest only upon his interest and ambition. If you wish to pass for a wise man, learn how to artfully disguise your true character.

XII.

On Statesmanship and Diplomacy.

Statesmanship can be reduced to three principles or maxims. The first is to maintain your
power, and, according to circumstances, to in-
crease and extend it. The second is to form
alliances only for your own advantage; and the
third is to command fear and respect even in
the most disastrous times.

First Principle. — On ascending the throne, I
examined my father's treasury: his great econ-
omy enabled me to conceive great projects.
Some time afterwards, I reviewed my troops, and
found them in a superb condition. After this
review, I returned to my coffers again, and took
out from them funds enough to double my
army.

As I had just doubled my power, it was not
natural that I should confine myself to preserving what I had; so I had soon decided to avail

myself of the first opportunity which might offer. Meanwhile, I kept my troops under arms and drilling constantly, and I did my best to draw the attention of all Europe to my movements. I renewed them every year, so as to appear more skilful, and, finally, I attained the end I had in view.

I astonished the world: all the powers, all the nations, thought every thing was over with them if they did not know how to move their heads, arms, and legs *à la Prussienne.*

All my officers and soldiers seemed to be worth twice as much when they saw they were imitated everywhere. When my troops had thus acquired a real advantage over all the others, I was solely occupied with examining what claims I might lay to various provinces.

Four principal points presented themselves foremost to my notice, — Silesia, Polish Prussia, the Dutch Guelders, and Swedish Pomerania. I fixed upon Silesia to begin with, because that country deserved my attention more than any other, and because circumstances were more favorable to me there.

I left to time the care of executing my designs on the other countries.

I will not demonstrate to you the validity of my claims to that province : I had them established by my orators. The Queen (of Austria) had her orators oppose and refute them, and we ended the dispute by a war.

But, to return to the circumstances : the following is the way they presented themselves : —

France wished to dispossess the house of Austria of the empire, — the very thing I wanted. France wanted to make the Elector of Bavaria emperor : I was delighted at it, because that could be done only at the Queen's expense.

Finally, the French conceived the noble project of going to the gates of Vienna; that was what I was waiting for, in order to possess myself of Silesia.*

Then, my dear nephew, have plenty of money, give your troops an air of superiority, wait for favorable circumstances, and you will be sure,

* By the battle of Molwitz, April 20, 1741, he obtained possession of three-fourths of Silesia. — *Translator's note.*

not only of preserving your kingdom, but of enlarging it.

There are unskilful statesmen who pretend that a State which has reached a certain point must no longer think of aggrandizing itself, because the system of equilibrium has almost fixed boundaries for each power.

I agree that the ambition of Louis XIV. came near costing France very dear, and I know how much anxiety my own ambition has given me: but I also remember, that, in her greatest misfortunes, France gave a crown and kept her conquered provinces; and you have just seen that I lost nothing in the terrible disaster which threatened me.

So, every thing depends upon circumstances and upon the courage of the conqueror.

Besides, you cannot know, my dear nephew, how important it is for a king and for a State government to depart from ordinary practices.

It will be only by extraordinary proceedings that you can overawe others and acquire fame.

Equilibrium is a word which has subjugated the whole world, because people thought it afforded constant possession ; but, in reality it is nothing but a mere word.

Europe is a family where there are too many bad brothers and relatives. I say furthermore, my dear nephew, that it is by despising this system that vast projects can be formed.

See the English! They have the mastery of the sea : that proud element no longer dares to bear vessels without their permission.

The result of all I have just said is that we must always try, and be well persuaded that every thing suits us ; only we must take care not to display our pretensions with vanity. Be especially particular to have constantly at your court two or three eloquent men, and leave the care of your justification to them.

Second Principle. — To form alliances for one's own advantage. That is a State maxim. No power is authorized to neglect it : thence follows this consequence, that we must break alliances when they are prejudicial to us.

In my first war against the queen, I abandoned the French at Prague, because by that bargain I gained Silesia (1742).

Even if I had accompanied them as far as Paris, they never would have given me as much.

A few years after, I united with them again, • because I was anxious to attempt the conquest of Bohemia, and I wanted to make myself sure of success. I neglected the French nation in order to ally with the one which offered me the ' best chances of final success.

When Prussia will have become more powerful, my dear nephew, she can assume an air of constancy and good faith, which, at most, is fit only for the greatest powers and for petty sovereigns.

I told you, my dear nephew, that the word *policy* signifies, almost *roguery*, or *rascality ;* and that is true. However, you will find people, very sincere on the subject, who have adopted certain systems of probity. So, you can risk every thing with your embassadors. I have had some who served me devotedly, and who, in order to discover a mystery, would have searched even in the pocket of a king.

Try especially to win those who have the gift

of expressing themselves in ambiguous terms and susceptible of a double meaning.

It will not even be improper for you to have political locksmiths and physicians: they will sometimes be of great service to you.*

I know by experience all the advantages that can be expected from the services which such persons may render.

Third Principle. — To make yourself feared and respected by your neighbors is the height of great statesmanship. You can reach your end by two different means: the first is to dispose of a real force, the second to know well how to use the force which you have.

We are not in the first case: that is why I have neglected nothing to be in the second case.

There are some powers who imagine that an embassy should always make a great deal of show. However, the Duke de Richelieu, † at

---

* That is, "locksmiths" to pick locks, or to open doors; and "physicians" to dispose of troublesome people who might be in the way. — *Translator's note.*

† RICHELIEU *(Louis F. A. Duplessis, Duke de)*, also known under the name of *Marshal de Richelieu*, was born March 13, 1696, died Aug. 8, 1788. He was the great nephew of the famous Cardinal de Richelieu, the founder of the French Academy. — *Note of the Translator.*

4

Vienna, did nothing but give a poor opinion of the French, because the Austrians thought that the whole nation was as affected as its representative. For my part, I maintain that more true regard is paid to the noble and elevated language in which an embassador expresses the opinions of his sovereign, than to the display of a few equipages. It is for this reason, that I no longer wish to have embassadors, but merely envoys. Besides, it is too difficult to find a suitable person to fill the first position, because it requires a man of noble birth, very wealthy, and who is thoroughly versed in statesmanship, while the last qualification is sufficient for an envoy or a minister plenipotentiary. By adopting this system, you will save enormous sums of money every year, and, nevertheless, your affairs will be transacted all the same.

However, there are cases, my dear nephew, in which embassies must be on a scale of great magnificence ; as, for instance, when one is about to give up diplomatic relations with a court, or to make a political or a matrimonial alliance. But embassies should always be regarded as ex-

traordinary.   In order to inspire your neighbors
with awe, let your actions be accompanied with
as much splendor as possible, and, above all, let
no one write any thing in your kingdom except
to extol your doings.

Never ask any thing weakly, but appear rather
to demand.   If some one is disrespectful towards
you, reserve your vengeance for a time when you
can obtain full satisfaction, and, especially, do
not fear that your glory will be diminished by
it; so much the worse for those of your subjects
who may have to suffer by it.

But here is the true point: all your neighbors
must be quite persuaded that you are afraid of
nothing, and that nothing can astonish you.
Try especially to have them believe that you are
a dangerous monarch, who knows no other principle than that which leads to glory.   And con-
trive also to have them well convinced that you
would rather lose two kingdoms, than not to
occupy a prominent place in history.

As those sentiments belong only to rare intel-
lects, they strike and astonish most of men; and
it is an idea, which, in the world, constitutes a
great monarch.

When a foreigner comes to your court, treat him with extreme urbanity and hospitality ; and try, particularly, to have him always with you : that is the surest means of concealing the defects of your government. If he is a military man, make your body-guard manœuvre in his presence, and command the regiment yourself. If he happens to be an author who has composed a work, let him see it on your table. If he is a merchant, listen kindly to all that he says, endeavor to gain his confidence, and to induce him to remain in your dominions.